ESCAPE FROM ALCATRAZ

ATTACK OF THE DRONES

BY MICHAEL DAHL

ILLUSTRATED BY PATRICIO CLAREY

Raintree is an imprint of Capstone Global Library Limited, a company incorporated in England and Wales having its registered office at 264 Banbury Road, Oxford, OX2 7DY – Registered company number: 6695582

www.raintree.co.uk
myorders@raintree.co.uk

Edited by Aaron J Sautter
Designed by Kay Fraser
Original illustrations © Capstone Global Library Limited 2020
Production by Katy LaVigne
Originated by Capstone Global Library Ltd
Printed and bound in India

ISBN: 978 1 4747 8493 1 (paperback)

British Library Cataloguing in Publication Data
A full catalogue record for this book is available from the British Library.

Acknowledgements
Design elements: Shutterstock: Agustina Camilion, A-Star, Dima Zel, Draw_Wing_Zen, Hybrid_Graphics, Metallic Citizen

CONTENTS

ERRO

PLATEAU of LENG

PHANTOM FOREST

POISON SEA

VULCAN MOUNTAINS

LAKE of GOLD

METAL MOON

DIAMOND MINES

MONSTER ZOO

PITS of NO RETURN

PRISON STRONGHOLDS

SWAMP of FLAME

SCARLET JUNGLE

PRISON ENERGY DRIVES

SPACE PORT PRISONER INTAKE

ABYSS of GIANTS

ZAK

THE PRISONERS

ZAK NINE

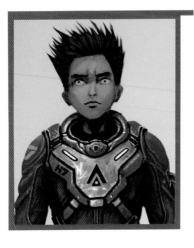

Zak is a teenage boy from Earth Base Zeta. He dreams of piloting a star fighter one day. Zak is very brave and is a quick thinker. But his enthusiasm often leads him into trouble.

ERRO

Erro is a teenage furling from the planet Quom. He has the fur, long tail, sharp eyes and claws of his species. Erro is often impatient with Zak's reckless ways. But he shares his friend's love of adventure.

THE PRISON PLANET

Alcatraz . . . there is no escape from this terrifying prison planet. It's filled with dungeons, traps, endless deserts and other dangers. Zak Nine and his alien friend, Erro, are trapped here. They had sneaked onto a ship hoping to see an awesome space battle. But the ship landed on Alcatraz instead. Now they have to work together if they ever hope to escape!

ERRO'S STORY . . . A JUNGLE HIDEOUT >>>

Zak and I are hiding from Alcatraz's robot guards in a thick, red jungle. The robots cannot follow us here. But we keep hearing many strange sounds. Zak thinks the guards are using attack drones to hunt us down. If that is true, it will not be long before they find us. . . . >>>>

CHAPTER ONE:
BUZZ!

This red jungle is endless. Zak and I have been hiding here for several days. Luckily the Alcatraz guards cannot follow us through the thick trees.

But there is still danger here. We have not seen any creatures in the jungle, but we can hear them. At night we hear weird bird cries in the dark.

At night we take turns sleeping.
We only sleep a few hours before we
start moving again.

BZZZZZ!

Huge horned insects fly among the jungle's giant flowers. The buzzing bugs are almost as big as us.

I point them out to Zak. "They look like your Earth buzz," I say.

"You mean *bees*," says Zak. "*Buzz* is the sound they make."

Bees? Buzz? What is the difference? I think.

"Your language is tricky," I say.

We watch the noisy insects flit among the big, bell-shaped flowers.

"Watch out for their stingers," says Zak. "They're huge!"

ZZZZZZZZZ!

We hear another buzzing sound overhead. But this sound does not come from the insects. It comes from high above the trees.

"Robot guards?" I ask.

"No – drones!" Zak shouts.

CHAPTER TWO:
UNDERFOOT

We run deeper into the jungle.
The trees' thick, red leaves crowd
out the light.

ZZZZZZZ!

"They are getting closer!" I warn.

I start running faster. The last
time drones chased us, they fired
lasers. I do not like laser blasters.

"Oooohhhhhh!" Zak cries out behind me.

I run back to find Zak lying on the ground. His eyes are shut tight with pain.

"Did a laser hit you?" I ask. "I cannot see any drones."

"My foot!" groans Zak.

"The laser hit your foot?"

"No!" he says. "My foot caught on a stupid root, and I fell."

Zak rubs his ankle. "I don't think I can run on it," he says.

Zak always sounds brave, but this time I see fear in his eyes.

"I can help," I say. "Hold on to my shoulder."

Zak shakes his head. "No. I'll only slow you down," he says.

The leaves suddenly start shaking overhead.

Oh no! I think. *The drones are here!*

CHAPTER THREE:
UNDER ATTACK!

But it is not the drones. Hundreds
of screeching, colourful birds suddenly
drop from the branches above us. Then
they fly deeper into the jungle.

"That is not normal," I tell Zak.
"Something must have scared them."

Bright lights flash between the leaves
above us.

KRRROOOOOSH!

A powerful laser beam hits the branch above us, and it bursts into flame.

"You were right," says Zak.
"The drones scared the birds. We
have to keep moving!"

Zak holds on to my shoulder as
we move through the trees.

"Many creatures live in this jungle," I tell my friend. "That should help fool the drones' sensors."

"Maybe. But few creatures can walk on two legs like us," Zak says.

"Then we have to hide our legs,"
I reply.

Zak snorts. "Right. Are you some sort
of magician, fur boy?"

My Quom eyes can see a large shape
ahead of us.

"No, Earth boy," I say. "But I grew
up in a jungle like this. I know how
things work."

ZZZZZZAAAATT!

Another laser blast barely misses us.

"Yeah? Well I know how lasers work," Zak replies. "Trust me, you don't want to find out."

We hide in the shadow of a large tree. Zak leans against the trunk.

Now he sees the same large shape that I do.

It is a large lake. Far out on the lake sits a huge flock of the colourful birds.

CHAPTER FOUR:
UNDER WATER

The tree suddenly shakes violently.

KRASSSH!

A burning branch falls next to us.

"Look!" Zak points at two shapes flying above us.

The drones have shiny metal bodies and short wings. Red and orange lights blink at both ends.

They remind me of the buzzing insects we saw before.

"Come on!" I yell, pulling Zak into the lake with me. "The water will hide us."

"We can't hide down there forever," says Zak. "We need to breathe!"

I look around and see more big, bell-like flowers growing by the water. I grab two of them and hand one to Zak.

"Quick! Put this over your head," I tell him.

We slip the flowers over our heads and stumble into the lake.

The large blossoms hold pockets of air. We can breathe as we sink deeper into the water.

"It's like a diving helmet!" says Zak.

"Yes, just breathe normally and keep swimming," I tell him.

CHAPTER FIVE:
FLIGHT OF FREEDOM

I pull Zak deeper into the lake.

ZHHHOOOOM!

More lasers slice through the water nearby. I feel warm bubbles swirling around me.

Just a little further, I tell myself. *We need to get close to those alien birds.*

The birds may be like the ones on Quom. When one flies, the others follow.

Then I hear a strange noise from under the water. It is the muffled roar of a thousand screaming birds. I swim up to the surface to see more.

The huge flock of alien birds rises into the sky. It swarms past the drones, confusing them. Dozens of the panicking birds crash into the buzzing aircraft.

Zak's head bobs up next to mine. We both watch as the damaged drones fall into the lake with a splash.

"That was awesome!" says Zak.

We both take a gulp of air and dive underwater with our flower helmets. We continue swimming towards the other side of the lake.

If we are lucky, we can escape before more deadly drones arrive. . . .

GLOSSARY

diving helmet large, round helmet worn over the head; usually used to supply air for a deep-sea diver

drone unmanned aircraft that is controlled from the ground

dungeon prison, usually underground

flit move lightly and quickly

jungle land thickly covered with trees, vines and bushes

laser thin, intense beam of light

panicking be in a state of extreme fear or terror

sensor device that can detect changes in the environment

species group of living things that share similar features

stinger sharp, pointy part of an animal that can be used to sting

TALK ABOUT IT

1. At the start of the story, Erro and Zak are taking turns sleeping as they hide from the Alcatraz guards. Do you think this is a wise choice? Explain your answer.

2. Erro confused the word "buzz" with the word "bees" in the story. Have you confused words with others that sound similar? Share some examples of words you think are confusing.

3. Erro wanted to run, but helped support Zak after he hurt his ankle. Talk about a time when you helped a friend in need, even though you might have wanted to do something else instead.

WRITE ABOUT IT

1. Many strange creatures live in planet Alcatraz's Scarlet Jungle. Use your imagination to create a list of creatures that might live there. Write a brief description for each.

2. Can you think of another way Zak and Erro could escape from the deadly drones? Write a new ending to the story using your own plans for the boys to escape.

ABOUT THE AUTHOR

Michael Dahl is the author of more than 300 books for
young readers, including the Library of Doom series.
He is a huge fan of Star Trek, Star Wars and Doctor
Who. He has a fear of closed-in spaces, but has visited
several prisons, dungeons and strongholds, both ancient
and modern. He made a daring escape from each one.
Luckily, the guards still haven't found him.

ABOUT THE ILLUSTRATOR

Patricio Clarey was born in 1978 in Argentina.
He graduated in fine arts at the School of Visual
Arts Martín Malharro, specializing in illustration and
graphic design. Patricio currently lives in Barcelona,
Spain, where he works as a freelance graphic designer
and illustrator. He has created several comics and
graphic novels, and his work has been featured in
several books and other publications.